Mr. Putter & Tabby
Drop the Ball

CYNTHIA RYLANT

Mr. Putter & Tabby
Drop the Ball

Illustrated by

ARTHUR HOWARD

Harcourt Children's Books

Houghton Mifflin Harcourt

Boston   New York   2013

For all the fans
—C.R.

For Rachel, Stephen, and Eli
—A.H.

Text copyright © 2013 by Cynthia Rylant
Illustrations copyright © 2013 by Arthur Howard

Harcourt Children's Books is an imprint of
Houghton Mifflin Harcourt Publishing Company.

www.hmhbooks.com

The illustrations in this book were done in pencil, watercolor,
and gouache on 250-gram cotton rag paper.
The text type was set in Berkeley Old Style Book.
The display type was set in Artcraft.

Library of Congress Cataloging-in-Publication Data
Rylant, Cynthia.
Mr. Putter & Tabby drop the ball / Cynthia Rylant ;
illustrated by Arthur Howard.
p. cm.
Summary: Mr. Putter and his cat Tabby take time off from napping to play
on the Yankee Doodle Dandies baseball team.
ISBN 978-0-15-205072-6
[1. Old age—Fiction. 2. Cats—Fiction. 3. Baseball—Fiction.] I. Howard, Arthur, illustrator.
II. Title. III. Title: Mister Putter & Tabby drop the ball.
IV. Title: Mr. Putter and Tabby drop the ball.
PZ7.R982Mscp 2013
[E]—dc23
2012046367

Manufactured in China
SCP 1 3 5 7 9 10 8 6 4 2
4500419053

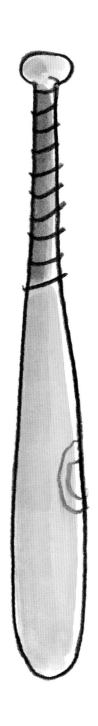

1
Baseball!

2
The Team!

3
The Dandies!

4
Drop the Ball!

5
What a Day!

1

Baseball!

Mr. Putter and his fine cat, Tabby,
loved to nap in the summertime.
They loved napping in the garden.
They loved napping on the porch.
They loved napping in the car.

"It seems that we nap all the time,"
Mr. Putter said to Tabby one day.
Tabby was old and her frisky days were over.

She loved napping.

"I think we need a sport," said Mr. Putter.

Tabby opened one eye.

"I think we need *baseball*," said Mr. Putter.
Tabby opened the other eye.
"I wonder where my old mitt is,"
said Mr. Putter.
He headed to the basement.
Tabby was wide awake now!

2
The Team!

Mr. Putter found his mitt.

"Now all we need is a team," he told Tabby.

Mr. Putter called his friend and neighbor,

Mrs. Teaberry.

Mrs. Teaberry would know about a team.
She was very sporty.
She even walked the Dog-A-Thon
with her good dog, Zeke.

"Of course there's a team!" said Mrs. Teaberry.
"It's called the Yankee Doodle Dandies."
"Am I too old to play?" asked Mr. Putter.
"Heavens, no," said Mrs. Teaberry,
handing Zeke a Sniffy Bone.
"You will feel *young* on that team."

"Will my *knees* feel young on that team?"
asked Mr. Putter.

"You are not too old, and neither am I,"
said Mrs. Teaberry. "We'll both play!"

Mr. Putter hung up the phone.

"I hope I'm not too old," he said to Tabby.

Tabby just purred.

To her, Mr. Putter was perfect.

3

The Dandies!

Mrs. Teaberry and Zeke arrived
in their baseball clothes.
"Let's go!" said Mrs. Teaberry.
They all drove to the ball field.

The Yankee Doodle Dandies
were in the middle of a game.
A batter was running for home.

Everyone waited and waited and waited.

"I'm feeling pretty young," said Mr. Putter.

"Let's go play," said Mrs. Teaberry.
She looked at Zeke.
"Stay," she said, patting Zeke's head.
Mr. Putter looked at Zeke.
No way, Mr. Putter thought.

He petted Tabby and went to play.

4

Drop the Ball!

The Yankee Doodle Dandies were very nice.
They let Mr. Putter and Mrs. Teaberry
play right away.
Mr. Putter took the outfield.
Mrs. Teaberry took shortstop.

The batter came up.

Swing and a miss. Swing and a miss.

Swing and a miss.

Hmm, thought Mr. Putter in the outfield.

I could be taking a nap.

Another batter came up.

Swing and a miss. Swing and a miss.

Swing and . . . *a ground ball to second!*

Mrs. Teaberry leaped into action!
She ran for the ball!
She reached for the ball!
Then . . .

GLOMP!

Zeke got the ball!

He was very proud.

He ran around and around in circles.

"Drop the ball, Zeke!" everyone yelled.

Zeke did not drop the ball.

The other teamed scored.

"Oh, dear," said Mrs. Teaberry.

Oh, boy, thought Mr. Putter.

Tabby purred in the dugout.
Baseball was fun!

5

What a Day!

Another batter came up.

Swing and a miss. Swing and a miss.

Swing and . . . *a ground ball to third!*

Mr. Putter couldn't watch.

GLOMP!

Zeke got the ball and ran in circles.

The other team scored again.

The Yankee Doodle Dandies were not happy.

They benched Zeke.

"*Stay,*" they said.

No way, thought Mr. Putter.

The score was tied 2–2.

If the other team scored again,

the Dandies would lose.

A batter came up.

Swing and a miss. Swing and a miss.

Swing and . . . *a hit to the outfield!*

Mr. Putter leaped into action!

He ran for the ball.

It was rolling, rolling . . .

He'd have to bend down to get the ball.

Mr. Putter tried to bend down.

But his knees said, *No way.*

The Dandies were about to lose!

But then . . .

GLOMP!

Zeke got the ball!

Zeke looked at Mr. Putter.

Mr. Putter looked at Zeke.

Then Zeke *jumped!*
He jumped and he put that ball
right into Mr. Putter's mitt!

Then Mr. Putter
THREW THAT BALL TO HOME!
And because the batter
was one hundred years old
and hadn't gotten there yet,
the Dandies *got him out!*
HOORAY!

The game ended in a tie.
The Dandies carried Zeke
on their shoulders,
and they gave Tabby a ride
in the peanuts box.

What a day!
Mr. Putter and Tabby
and Mrs. Teaberry and Zeke
ate ten free bags of peanuts
and drank three gallons of water.

Then they all found a nice spot
in the dugout and took a long nap.
Zeke's feet twitched a lot.
But he couldn't help it—
he was still in the game!